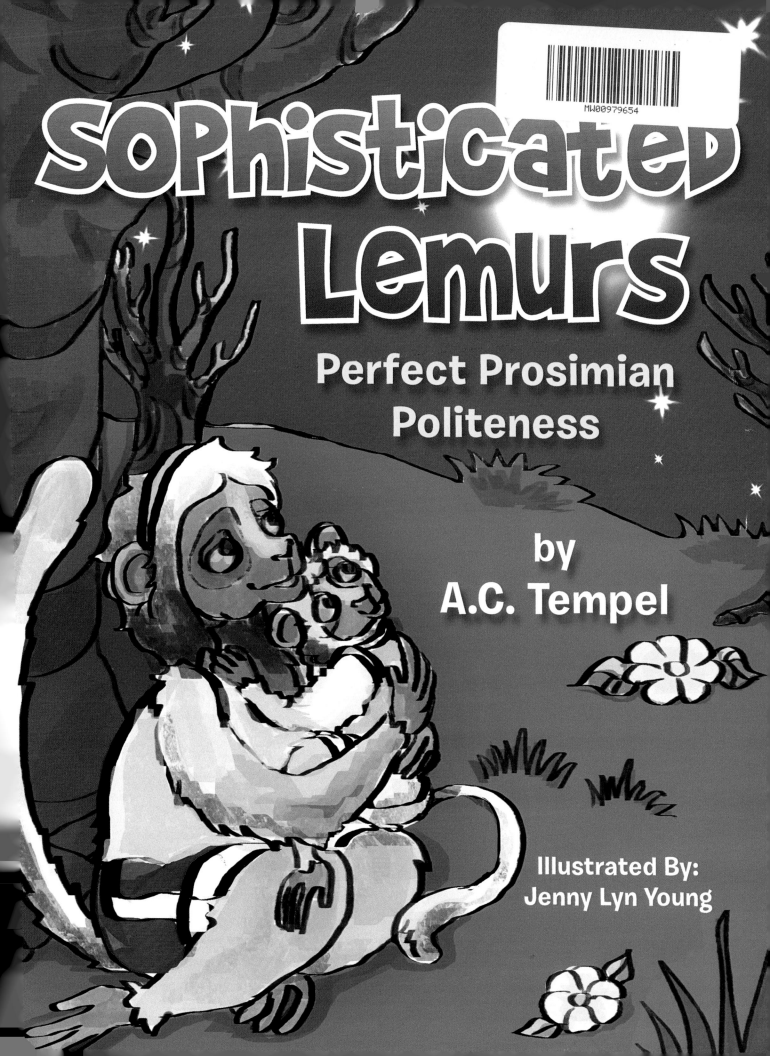

SOPHISTICATED Lemurs

Perfect Prosimian Politeness

by
A.C. Tempel

Illustrated By:
Jenny Lyn Young

To order additional copies of this book, contact:
Xlibris LLC
1-888-795-4274
www.Xlibris.com
Orders@Xlibris.com

To Logan.

My Beautiful Son and Little Gentleman.
May You ALWAYS See Wonder in the World!

LEMURS, LEMURS... JUMPING AROUND...
SOPHISTICATED LEMURS ALL SIT DOWN!

LEMURS, LEMURS SCREECH AND SHOUT...
SOPHISTICATED LEMURS ARE QUIET WHEN OUT!

LEMURS, LEMURS STUFF THEIR FACE...
SOPHISTICATED LEMURS ALWAYS SAY GRACE!

LEMURS, LEMURS KICK AND SCREAM...
SOPHISTICATED LEMURS LOVE TO BE CLEAN!
(BUBBLE BUBBLE)

LEMURS, LEMURS DIG UP THEIR NOSE...
SOPHISTICATED LEMURS PREFER TISSUE,
I SUPPOSE!

LEMURS, LEMURS PUSH AND SQUIRM...
SOPHISTICATED LEMURS WAIT THEIR TURN!

LEMURS, LEMURS... JUMP OUT OF BED...
SOPHISTICATED LEMURS REST THEIR HEAD.

LEMURS BIG AND LEMURS SMALL, GOODNIGHT-
SLEEP TIGHT, WE LOVE YOU ALL!

WILD AND WONDERFUL
FUN FACTS ABOUT OUR PROSIMIAN FRIENDS

Did you know.....

- The word lemur means spirits of the night.

- Lemurs are a type of primate called prosimian. This literally means before ape. Other prosimians include: lorises, bushbabies, and tarsiers. They all have 10 fingers and 10 toes with nails, not claws. They also have opposable thumbs. Their eyes are forward-facing and they have large brains relative to their size.

- Lemurs live only on the island of Madagascar and some are found in the Comoro Islands in South East Asia.

- The smallest species (Dwarf Lemur) weighs in at only around 10 grams (ex. 4 pennies) while the largest (Indri) can weigh up to 15 lbs.

- Lemurs are very social and live in family groups in which the females are dominant over the males. Girls Rule!

- Most lemurs live their lives in trees, but some, such as the ring-tail prefer the ground.

- Most species are nocturnal, meaning they are active during the night. However, it isn't uncommon to see some active during the day (diurnal).

- Lemurs have something called a "tooth comb" which they use for grooming themselves and each other.

- Many species have scent glands used for marking their territory. Many of these glands are found on their necks, top of heads, chest, and forearms. Think of it as natural perfume which tells other lemurs, "I was here!"

- Lemurs have a huge array of calls, squeaks, and other vocalizations to communicate with each other. These sounds are often passed down from their parents to their young.

- Although the tail of a lemur is usually longer than it's body, it is not prehensile. They can't hang from trees with it like a opossum or pangolin. The Indri does not have a tail.

- Lemurs are excellent jumpers! For example, the Coquerel Sifaka, can jump up to 20 feet horizontally! Now that is worth an Olympic gold metal.

- Many lemur species feed on flowers, fruits, bark, and leaves. The Aye Aye loves to dine on insect larvae and has a special technique for detecting its dinner. The Aye Aye has very large ears and can hear incredibly well. They also have a long, slender middle finger that can be used to rapidly tap on branches of trees to locate the larvae. They listen very carefully, once found, the lemur takes its teeth and bites off chucks of wood to get its supper. They use their long finger to dig out the larvae and scoop it up! YUMMY

- Because of its unique appearance, the Aye Aye is believed by natives of Madagascar to be evil or a bad omen. Sadly, many are hunted and killed on the spot. This is NOT true. On-going education and conservation is essential to save these and all species which are endangered and threatened to extinction.

- The lemur's only natural predator is the fossa and humans. Otherwise, the general lifespan in the wild can be 18 years.

**DUKE PRIMATE CENTER, Durham, North Carolina is the largest conservation/ research facility in the world outside Madagascar where you can view lemurs and learn more about them and other prosimians. They have the largest variety of species in captivity in the United States. A portion of all sales of this book, is donated to Duke Primate Center to encourage on-going education to the public, research, and the conservation of these beautiful animals.

PLEASE USE YOUR CREATIVITY TO COLOR YOUR LEMUR AND DISPLAY YOUR ARTWORK!

Edwards Brothers Malloy
Thorofare, NJ USA
January 20, 2014